I'm a
Gluten-Sniffing
Service Dog

Michal Babay
illustrated by **Ela Śmietanka**

Albert Whitman & Company
Chicago, Illinois

Every dog needs a person, and Alice is mine.

Almost.

I just have to graduate from training school, then we'll be together all the time.

Alice is great at ear scratching and playing fetch.

I can't wait to become her super-sniffing service dog!

But visiting day's over.
And with the slam of a car door, she's gone.
Again.
Come baaaaaaaaaaack!

At least she gave me her sweatshirt,
to sniff when I'm lonely.
Sniff.
Sniff.
Yup.
Smells like Alice.

I'm going to train my tail off so we can…
Hold on. Where's my tail?
"Chewie! Ready to work?"
Phew. Found it. Ready!
One last peek at the empty parking lot,
and then back to training.

"Check!"
Sniff.
Sniff.
Sugar, milk, butter, and...gluten!
Gluten is a protein found in certain grains, and
even a small amount can make Alice sick because
she has celiac disease,
   so...

Circle, circle.
ALERT!
Oh yeah, nailed it.
My nose *always* knows.

Becoming a service dog is hard work.
I practice every day.

"Check!"
Sniff.
Sniff.
Down.
ALL CLEAR!
No gluten in *this* cheese.

"Check!"
Sniff.
Sniff.
Circle, circle.
ALERT!
Don't eat the salad dressing!

"Check!"
Sniff.
Sni—
Bug! On my nose!
In the air! On the
grass! Buuuuuuuug!
Oops.

Time-out on my mat.
Turns out, service dogs can't chase bugs while on duty.
There's so much to remember.
Or forget.
I wish Alice were here to rub my belly.
I snuggle her sweatshirt.
Alice believes in me.
But...

Can I keep her safe?
Gluten hides *everywhere*—in licorice, vitamins,
even DOG food!
What if I mess up?

Or forget my training?
Or—
BIRD!
—get distracted?
I miss my friend, my ear
scratcher, my girl.

The next morning, training
keeps me busy.
After breakfast…
SNAP!
On goes my vest.

Time to work!
I do lots of sniff training.
Plus searching, sitting, staying,
and coming when called.
Playtime, rest, and then…

CLICK!
On goes my leash.
Field-trip time!
I practice in markets:
"Check!"

SERVICE
DOG
IN TRAINING

Sniff.
Sniff.
Circle, circle.
ALERT!

"Check!"
Sniff.
Sniff.
Down.
ALL CLEAR on the soap!

At parks:
"Heel!"
"Sit!"
"Down!"

And in restaurants:

"Stay!"

"Good boy."

Yes! In my vest, I'm the best!
Wait, is that PIZZA on the sidewalk?
Just. Gonna. Scoot. Over. A. Little...

"Chewie, STAY!"

Something's different today.
What's happening?
Everyone's graduating, and going home
with their person.
Everyone...
but me.
*Guys? Hello? Super-Sniffing Poodle
ready for action! Let's go!*

Oh.
Turns out, I can't graduate until
I've mastered one more skill.
The hardest of all—
staying focused.
Even when—
Bug!
Bird!
TAIL!

Then one day...
Sniff.
Sniff.
I smell Alice!

She's back!
I grab a ball and race over, but Alice just sits.
And hugs me.
"Chewie, I need you. I keep getting sick and can't go anywhere now. Not to parties or even *school*. I just want to feel normal again, but nothing's safe without you. Please graduate, Chewie. Please."
My heart flops.
Alice *sounds* like I *feel* when our sweatshirt's missing.

But I've been trained for this.
A soft ear lick, then "cover."
And I don't move an inch, even when
Alice's tears tickle my nose.
She needs me.
And I need her.
Because we're partners.
Almost.

IT'S TIME TO FOCUS!
This week, Alice stays.
We train together.

Now, I'm a poodle on task, on a mission,
and ignoring all distractions.

At the park...
*I can't play! Not now.
Maybe later.*

the mall...*Hot dog on the
ground. Hot dooooooooog.
Bye-bye, hot dog. I hope
someone else eats you.*

even at the zoo…**Monkeys! Rhinos! Peacocks! I'm not looooooooking.**

I check popcorn, chips, ice cream, and other tempting treats.

With Alice by my side, I stay focused.

Until *finally*…

We're graduating!
It's OUR turn now!
Best. Day. Ever.

Bring on the strange house and all these new scents.
Sniff, sniff. Whoa, who are YOU?
Everything's perfect—I can always smell Alice.

Now, Alice and I stick
together like glue.
Gluten-free glue.
"Check!"
Sniff.
Sniff.

ALL CLEAR!
I check everything *before* she uses it.
No more stomach pains or headaches
when I'm on the job!
Just face licks,
and laughter.

Slowly, we go out more—
to movies, birthday parties, and finally…
school.
Backpacks make the BEST pillows!

Because NOW we're partners.
Alice calls me her doggy super sniffer and lifesaver.
I call her...
my girl.

Author's Note

This book is based on the true story of my daughter, Elina, and her gluten detection service dog, Chewie.

Chewie lives and works with Elina. This is because, just like Alice, Elina has celiac disease, and it raged out of control for many years. Eventually, the pains got so bad that she couldn't go anywhere. Not even to school! It took many doctor and hospital visits, a highly targeted "Gluten Contamination Elimination Diet" (she couldn't eat almost anything processed in a factory), and more than three months of steroids, but at sixteen years old, Elina finally regained her health.

Now Chewie helps protect her from hidden gluten, and provides emotional support as well.

Chewie was trained by Jillian Skalky from Creating New Tails.

Information on Celiac Disease for Parents and Caregivers

Celiac disease is a serious autoimmune condition. For people with celiac disease, ingesting gluten triggers a reaction in their small intestine. Over time, this damages the intestine's lining and prevents it from absorbing some nutrients. If left untreated, celiac disease can cause many other health issues.

Symptoms range from asymptomatic (silent celiac) to, more commonly, diarrhea, stomach pain, and bloating, but may also include numerous other issues. Given the variation in symptoms, it's important to call your doctor if you suspect celiac as a possibility.

Currently, there is no cure for celiac disease. The only treatment is a strict one-hundred-percent-gluten-free diet for life. Since gluten is a protein found in wheat, rye, and barley, people with celiac must avoid foods such as pasta, bread, cookies, and crackers unless they are specifically made to be gluten free. But gluten is tricky! It also hides in unexpected places, like soy sauce, candy bars, medications, and lip balms. To completely avoid gluten, you must become an expert at reading labels.

The US Food and Drug Administration approves gluten-free labeling on foods up to 20 parts per million. But for some people with celiac disease, 20 ppm may still be too much. Gluten detection dogs, like Chewie, are trained to detect gluten down to 2 parts per million to help sensitive people know which foods and products are safe for them.

To learn more about celiac, visit online resources like the Celiac Disease Foundation (celiac.org), the National Celiac Association (nationalceliac.org), the Mayo Clinic (www.mayoclinic.org), and the National Institute of Diabetes and Digestive and Kidney Diseases (www.niddk.nih.gov).

For Shalom, Elina, Daniel, and Liora—I love you, always
and forever. Together we can conquer anything.
And to everyone struggling with an invisible disease,
you're not alone. We see you.—MB

For my neighbors, with whom I walk in the mountains—EŚ

A special thank you to Dr. Deborah Rubin
for always being our partner and advocate. Thank you
for reviewing the celiac information included here.

Library of Congress Cataloging-in-Publication data
is on file with the publisher.
Text copyright © 2021 by Michal Babay
Illustrations copyright © 2021 by Albert Whitman & Company
Illustrations by Ela Śmietanka
First published in the United States of America in 2021
by Albert Whitman & Company
ISBN 978-0-8075-3631-5 (hardcover)
ISBN 978-0-8075-3646-9 (ebook)
Printed in China
10 9 8 7 6 5 4 3 2 1 WKT 24 23 22 21 20

Design by Rick DeMonico

For more information about Albert Whitman & Company,
visit our website at www.albertwhitman.com.